MEG and MOG

for Loveday

MEG and MOG

by Helen Nicoll
and Jan Pieńkowski

PUFFIN BOOKS

Once upon a time
there was a witch
called Meg

At midnight
the owl hooted 3 times
and woke her up

She got out of bed
to dress for
the spell party

She
put
on

her black
stockings

her big
black shoes

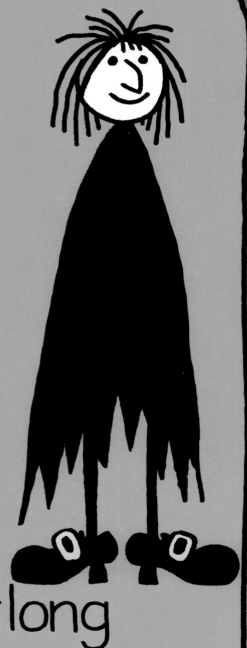

her long
black cloak

and her tall
black hat

In the kitchen
lay her big
striped cat Mog
He was
fast asleep

She trod on Mog's tail

She took out
of her cupboard

3 eggs

a kipper

Bread

Cocoa

MILK

JAM

At 1 o'clock she got her broomstick her cauldron and a spider

and she flew up the chimney with Mog

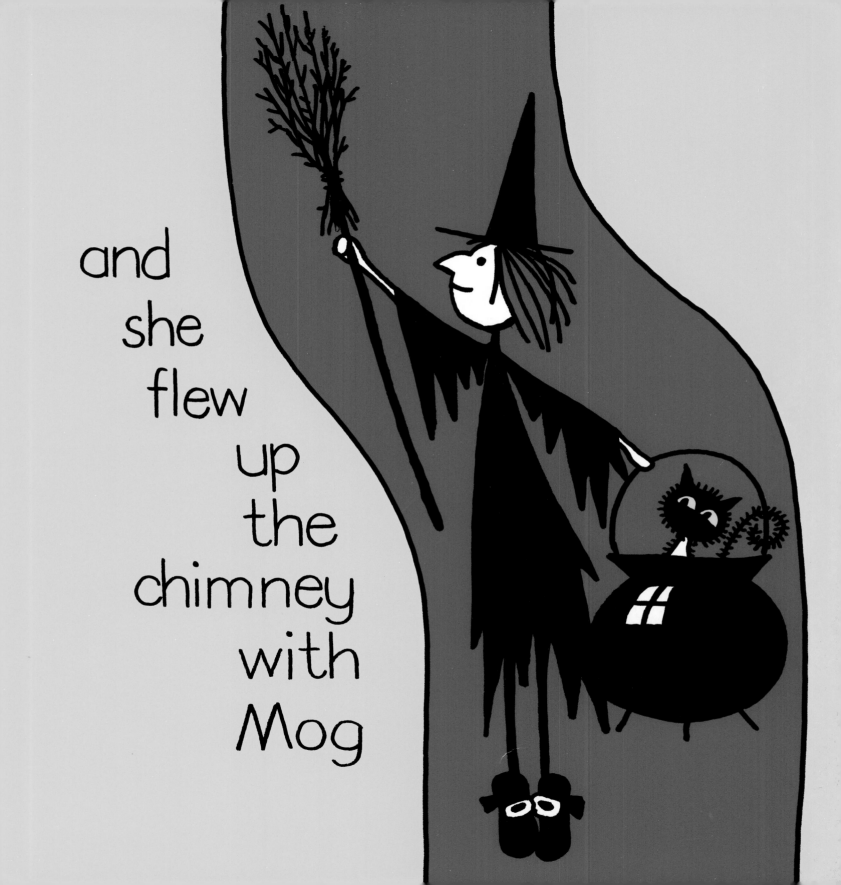

Up in the sky

she met her friends
going to the party
Bess

Jess

Tess

and

Cress

They landed on a hill
in the moonlight
to make the spell

Each of them
had brought something
to put in the cauldron

ABRACAD

They all
stirred the cauldron
as they chanted
their spell

There was
a flash
and a bang

Something had gone wrong

Bess, Jess,
Tess and Cress
all changed into mice
and Mog chased them

Goodbye!

PUFFIN BOOKS
Published by the Penguin Group: London, New York, Australia, Canada,
India, Ireland, New Zealand and South Africa
Penguin Books Ltd, Registered Offices: 80 Strand, London WC2R 0RL, England
puffinbooks.com
First published by William Heinemann Ltd 1972
Published in Puffin Books 1975
This edition published in Puffin Books 2012
001 - 10 9 8 7 6 5 4 3 2 1
Text copyright © Helen Nicoll, 1972
Illustrations copyright © Jan Pieńkowski, 1972
Story and characters copyright © Helen Nicoll and Jan Pieńkowski, 1972
All rights reserved. The moral right of Helen Nicoll and Jan Pieńkowski has been asserted
Lettering by Caroline Austin
Made and printed in China   ISBN: 978-0-141-34367-9